A TONY FLANER MYSTERY

THE
KNICKKNACK
CASE

Copyright © 2021 by Johnny Worthen

Cover design © 2021 by Dandelion Ink, LLC.
Cover design by Rebecacovers.

ISBN-978-1-7331072-5-9 (paperback)
ISBN-978-1-7331072-4-2 (ebook)

Second paperback edition: May 2021

Library of Congress Control Number: 2020900961

For the fans.

ALSO BY JOHNNY WORTHEN

TONY FLANER MYSTERIES
The Finger Trap
The Knickknack Case (A Novella)
Thicker Than Water
In the Wake of Captain Lord
The Counterfeit Connection

OTHER EXCELLENT BOOKS
Eleanor, The Unseen Book 1
Celeste, The Unseen Book 2
David, The Unseen Book 3
The Brand Demand
Beatrysel
Dr. Stuart's Heart
What Immortal Hand

A TONY FLANER MYSTERY

THE KNICKKNACK CASE

JOHNNY WORTHEN

DANDELION INK

FORWARD

Since Tony had to step out of the published world for a while, returning now gloriously with Dandelion Ink, he and I decided to write up this story and dedicate it to the many fans who patiently waited for our return.

This book can be enjoyed at anytime, home by a fire, on an airplane, stopped at a street light as a yellow Hummer leans on the horn to get you to move. It stands alone as pretty much all of Tony's books do, however, for the purist, it does occupy a specific place in the Cannon of Flaner®. In Tony's timeline of cases, this little adventure, THE KNICKKNACK CASE, happens between Chapters Forty-Four and Forty-Five of THE FINGER TRAP. In Chapter Forty-Five, the denouement of the book, you'll remember Tony mentioned this case in passing as a reference to his interest in staying on a career path. So, in a way, this novella is Flaner Book #1½ or maybe .9? Math isn't our strongpoint, but I think you'll get it. You're obviously an intelligent person with excellent taste.

Therefore, enjoy the story.

Thanks everyone. This book is for you.

—Johnny and Tony

CHAPTER ONE

It was a mess. It was dead.

I peeked through the hole into a desert wasteland of moistureless, lifeless sticks, pebbles, and crumbling moss. Decay. It was supposed to be an Eden, a self-contained system of life. Soil, nutrients—green and alive, recycled water and ongoing solar power beneath a dome of clear plastic. It was supposed to be my own created paradise. Complete. Whole and unending, but now it was just another short-lived hobby taking up space in my home and heart.

I'd made the terrarium out of a five-gallon water jug stolen from somewhere. I put in dirt, water, mushroom spores, and assorted earthy substances, but it hadn't worked. I never figured out why. Didn't give it enough effort to find out, I guess. I got distracted by another hobby after putting in my eighty percent effort and then deserted it in the basement. I hadn't seen it or thought about it in over ten years, but now it filled me with memories of scraping scum off river rocks, researching Amazonian ferns and feeling the power of playing God.

I put it in the pile of things to throw away, imagining for a moment some miniature silver-faced maniac demanding I witness him as he throws himself off a moving vehicle with a spear. Probably a Matchbox car. Could be a Hot Wheels, either one would fit. I had some of those around here somewhere.

When we divorced, my wife, in her own organized way, transferred all my stuff from the old house to this new one of mine. I had a lot, and, like now, I'd been unable to part with anything. I'd spent days in the old basement doing exactly what I was doing now, going through physical reminders of my past, feeling waves of nostalgia and sentimentality with each re-discovered treasure chasing keep or discard, life or death for each.

Nancy—that's my ex—told me from her real estate experience that a move is as good as a fire for getting rid of old stuff. Knowing that my stuff was made of asbestos, she made sure that my new house had a basement. Smart woman. She married me, didn't she? And divorced me.

I'd lived in this new house for months, and every third day or so I'd go down the stairs to the aforementioned basement turned storage unit and try to simplify. It was not going well. The stack of things to throw away was decidedly shorter than the stack of things I couldn't do without, like the toothpick castle siege diorama with working catapult and drawbridge, the *Love Boat* publicity pictures, and VHS recordings of *Seinfeld*.

I heard the doorbell. It wasn't Girl Scout season, so I ignored it.

There's a rule that if you haven't touched a thing or thought of a thing in two years, you don't need the thing. I remembered the rule and then dismissed it with Picasso's theorem: "Learn the rules like a pro so you can break them like an artist." Ha! I was an artist! Not a weak-willed sentimental hoarder with the attention span of … Huh … wait …I wonder if that could be a squirrel at the door. It was cold outside. January. Maybe they were going door to door to ask people for their leftover holiday nuts, fruitcakes, and god-awful candy canes. Charity begins at home.

The bell rang again, pulling me back to the basement.

I was a bachelor home-owning detective now, which meant vacuuming was optional, cinder blocks were chic, and I didn't have to answer the door if I didn't feel like it. My new life seemed stunningly similar to my old life, when I was teenager, or a freshman in college. Full of attitude and carbs. Déjà vu. Here I was re-living the irresponsibility that Nancy had stolen from me. Maturity is overrated.

Bell again. Knocking now.

A new life and a new house, but hell if I'd started fresh. Look at all this stuff. How the hell has this shit followed me around all these years? Why didn't someone tell me this was unhealthy? Okay, they did. Why didn't someone tell me loudly and constantly that I was approaching near psychotic levels of hoarding

2

with my never-ending flights of new interests? Okay, maybe that happened, too. But why didn't they do an intervention? Well, I mean a second intervention. One that worked.

Who stays at a door ringing and knocking for ten minutes? Two is unusual. Five is stalker-level. Ten is your house is on fire.

Sniffing for smoke, I moved the terrarium off the junk pile and back to the keep pile, thinking the grimy jug could come in handy to carry guzzoline after the Water Wars. You never know.

I stretched and remembered the time of my life when plastic jugs and slimy mud were the order of the day. Then I went upstairs, trying to remember where I'd put the fire extinguisher.

The knocking was louder, persistent but not panicked. The tenacity should have alerted me that it was an official visit. I call myself a detective. That was a clue. Part of my trade, like week-old hot dogs for gas-station Grab'n Go attendants. They're always there. But I was distracted and didn't put any of it together until I looked out the peephole. Only then, seeing the uniformed man outside set against the snowy yard, did I recognize that I'd missed a clue.

"Fuck," I said out loud. Too loud.

"Mr. Flaner?" came the voice.

"Do you have a warrant?" I called through the door.

"No. I'm Charlie, your mailman."

I looked again. Ah, yes, the uniform was different. Public servant blue, not stormtrooper black. No gun, but I did see pepper spray.

"Do I have to sign for something?"

"No. But I have a message for you."

"How do I know you really are a mailman?"

I saw a confused and frustrated look on the man's face. Then he lifted up a bundle of letters and waved them at the peephole. I saw bruised knuckles on his fingers and wondered if he'd left blood on my door. Who'd clean that up?

"Your story checks out." I opened the door.

"Are you moving?" he said, seeing the state of my living room, boxes and baubles, bubble wrap, and Styrofoam peanuts like Christmas snow.

3

"Moving in," I said.

"But you've been here for months."

"Your point?"

"Eh, yeah, sorry. Can I move those Chinese takeout cartons and sit down? I'm a little cold and tired."

"Which ones?"

"The ones there on the couch."

"Take the easy chair," I said. "It's more comfortable."

Gentleman host that I am, I let my mailman into my holocaust of a living room and watched as he shifted two-day-old takeout to an overflowing coffee table. He moved the statue of Thoth and piled them atop a pizza box.

He was a fit but older man. I put him in his sixties, maybe higher. Past retirement age in a civilized country but needing to "stay busy" in America so he wouldn't starve.

"Come the revolution!" I said.

"Excuse me?" said Charlie, my mailman.

"Nothing. Never mind. Want some coffee?"

"Do you have a clean mug?"

"Of course." I went to the kitchen and washed a mug, scraping out something tan with a spoon smelling like peanut butter. I poured coffee and microwaved it to smoldering tepid.

"Black?" I asked.

"Sure." I heard the sound of something sliding off something and landing on something else.

"Is this an official visit?"

"It's my day off," he said. "I'm doing a favor for a friend of mine. The mail I just brought up from your box."

"Why the uniform?"

"So you know I was who I said I was."

I came back in and offered him the mug.

He looked at it with wide eyes. I'd grabbed one of my heat-sensitive burlesque coffee mugs. It had a picture of a 1940s pinup girl whose clothes would vanish when the cup got hot. He averted his eyes as Betty Page revealed her assets.

"So you're my mailman?"

"Yes. We've talked a few times."

4

"Okay."

"Most people don't recognize me out of my uniform."

I nodded. "Makes sense."

"Or outside of my truck."

"That's it."

"But I really am your mailman." He gave me the stack of letters. "Here's your mail," he said. "About five days' worth, I think."

"Sounds about right," I said. "I've been busy unpacking." He glanced around at the mess as I took the mail and added it to the stack of unopened letters on the sideboard.

"Are you still a detective?"

"Hell yeah. Got my license and everything. But wait. How did you know that?"

"I read the paper."

"Ahhhh …"

"And you told me."

"I see. Well done. Very observant."

"Have you been drinking this morning?"

"Me? No. Why? Are you buying?"

He took a deep breath and sipped coffee until only Betty's thighs showed.

"I'm here for a friend. Mrs. Dewinter."

"She's in trouble?"

"She has a problem."

"Is D'Artagnan involved? Does the archbishop know?"

"What?"

"Who's Mrs. Dewinter?"

"She's a widow who lives a couple blocks over. I've known her for years. Been delivering her mail for thirty years at least. I'd say we're friends."

"She's a widow?"

"Yes."

"And she wants to know who killed her husband?"

"He died of a heart attack."

"Recently and suspiciously?"

"Eighteen years ago. Congenital."

"I think we're getting ahead of ourselves."

"We?"

I moved a chop suey carton to the floor and sat on the couch. "Maybe you should tell me what's going on. Start at the very beginning. It's a very good place to start."

"The Sound of Music."

"Do re me. Re me good."

"Maybe this was a mistake."

"Mrs. Dewinter has a problem," I said. "You want to help her. You need my help. Thus e pluribus unum, you're here to enlist me."

"Yes."

"So tell me about it."

"Someone's been stealing from her."

"Why not go to the police?"

"It's complicated."

"Well if there's one thing I am, it's complicated."

"Can you help her? Are you busy?" Another glance at the room.

"Actually, I am in between cases." My last case had been a marital infidelity sleaze fest where I had to fumigate my shoes for all the muck I'd had to kick up. On paper it paid well, but now there was the divorce, and the funds were frozen for the foreseeable future. A little money couldn't hurt. I was well off because of an allowance Nancy had set up for me, but I was going to need new terrarium supplies, maritime-themed picture frames for Captain Stubing, and a VHS player. Do they still make those?

"Tell me about it," I said.

"Let me take you to see Amelia—Mrs. Dewinter."

"Can I drive your mail truck?"

"No."

"Well, shit. How about the siren? Can I turn on the siren?"

"Sure," he said. "If you can find the switch, you can turn on the siren."

"Neat!"

CHAPTER TWO

There was no siren button in the mail truck. The closest thing I found were the hazard flashers, and I made us drive with them on the whole way.

It was freaky to sit on the driver's side and not have a steering wheel. I liked how people just drove around us even though we were going thirty miles per hour.

"Is it kosher for you to be using your truck on your day off?"

"No," said Charlie.

"Well, okay then."

The roads were dry from the snowplows, salt-caked white, but the gutters were black in sooty slush. The grayscale of a Utah winter. Mid-January.

We didn't have far to go. I was just about to comment on how quickly and efficiently the heater turned the cab from fridge to toaster when we pulled up to an old rambler a couple blocks from my house. Unlike mine, someone had shoveled her snow. Charlie pulled into the driveway and we got out.

Charlie, my mailman, knocked on the door and then opened it without waiting for a reply.

I raised an eyebrow.

He shrugged.

It was warm inside. Not too hot and not too cold. Just right. I followed Charlie's lead and took my shoes off by the door sniffing for porridge.

"Amelia?" he called. "It's me, Charlie. I brought that detective I told you about."

"Be right out," came a voice from deeper in the house.

The relationship I was witnessing was kind of weird. What kind of mailman walks into your house and calls you by first name? Suspicions roiled up in my mind, and I considered how best to tactfully probe them.

"So are you sleeping with Amelia?" I asked.

The question was shocking. Neither one of us could believe I'd actually asked it. I was more used to such ill manners and recovered first.

"It's not like it hasn't happened before," I said. "I have seen lots of movies about mailmen and lonely woman in all kinds of positions."

"Mr. Flaner—"

"Call me Tony. Maybe I should call you Special Delivery."

"What? No. No no no. Amelia's a friend of mine. People make friends, you know."

"Uh-huh. I know."

"She's been on my route forever. After her husband died, I made it my business to check up on her. That's all. Wellness checks. It's not like her grandkids ever look in on her."

His face was red with embarrassment, rage, or temperature differential. I assumed all three.

"Hello, Charlie," said a slim woman with big hair. She wore a sea-foam caftan with blue swirls and a V-neck that moved silkily as she moved. She came up to Charlie and kissed him on the cheek. His face went strawberry.

He cleared his throat and I noticed a wedding ring on his finger because he pushed it into my face.

"What's that about?" she said. "Oh, I get it. No, Mr. Flaner, Charlie and I are not an item. We're just old friends."

"Friends," he said and wiggled his finger.

"Mr. Flaner, I'm Amelia Dewinter," she said. "You're very kind to come. Would you like to sit down?"

She gestured to the living room where I could see the usual array of seldom-used furniture items—couch, love seat, end table, coffee table, shelves of knickknacks. Lots of shelves. Lots. Lots of knickknacks. Lots and lots and lots of knickknacks.

In our stocking feet, we followed her to the couch. My big toe poked out and checked the surroundings before trying and failing to retreat back into its cotton home.

I took a seat and admired all the tchotchkes. I was about

to comment on her collections when I felt my ears grow hot and my heart race. This is what organized hoarding looks like, I thought. This is the very state I was striving for in my house. It was not a good look. Everything was dusted and neat, but I could not find a single square inch of open table-top, shelf space, or floor not necessary for walking that did not have some item occupying the space. Some things, like a plastic model airplane, a B52 made from the classic Revell kit—I have one—hung from fishing line and floated in the only space available, that between floor and ceiling.

She read my mind, or maybe my face, the horror and little yelp of self-reflection, and said, "Yes, I know. An old lady's house, full of memories and memorabilia. Every piece has a history and a value. Even the house, even Charlie—all mean something to me, Mr. Flaner. I'm a sentimental old woman, and someone is taking advantage of that."

"Who?" I said.

"I think it's a grandson-in-law."

She was a handsome woman. She wore eye makeup— shadow, liner, false lashes from a time before I was born, lipstick, a touch of blush. No base. She didn't hide, but neither did she accent her deep age lines. Using what I know about human aging patterns, and seeing her face on black and white pictures with a man standing next to a real B52, I figured her to be in her nineties. She didn't look a day over eighty-five and acted more like thirty-five. She moved slowly, but her eyes were sharp and keen. They had to be to arrange that big hair into such a perfect hive, and this house into such perfect clutter.

Behind her in the kitchen I could see the motif of sentimental adoration continued with plates on the walls and spice racks—plural. I shuddered.

"Is it too cold in here?" she asked. "I'm in thermals. I don't get many guests."

"I'm fine."

"I'm married," said Charlie.

"I used to be," said I.

"Are you trying to date Charlie, Mr. Flaner?"

I took a long appraising look at the mailman and watched his cheeks redden again. "No. He's married. Tell me what's got you worried, Mrs. Dewinter."

She picked up a porcelain pig off the end table, blew invisible dust off it and spoke as if it was passing her the answers. "My husband died a few years ago. My son and his wife live in Arizona. They've told me it's the best place to retire, but, like I said, this place has sentimental value."

The pig was put back. The story was taken up by a snow globe.

"My grandkids live in town. They don't visit much, but when they do, things go missing."

"They're robbing you?"

"Maybe."

"What else could it be?" said Charlie.

"Verne. He might be taking my things and hiding them. He used to tease me about it."

"Who's Verne?"

"Amelia's late husband," said Charlie.

"Ah," I said. "Go on."

A portrait of a child at school.

"Paulie—that's my son—had two girls, Eliza and Jennifer. We call them Lizzie and Jenni. Lizzie's first husband is Hydyn. Jenni's is Eddie. Both are no-accounts."

"They're remarried?"

"Not yet."

"Ah."

"They're both addicts."

"Meth? Opioids?"

"Video games."

"Ah."

"And gambling."

"Both do both?"

"Eddie is the vidiot, Hydyn is the loser. Both are losers, really. Why those girls married those boys is beyond me."

"What did they steal?" I asked, hoping I wouldn't blurt out something like 'How the hell did you ever notice it was gone?'

"There was a Lladró statue I was very fond of. A girl with an umbrella."

"Valuable?"

She nodded. "A couple hundred at least. Maybe more. Probably more. It was on that shelf." She pointed to a wall.

"Which shelf?"

"The second from the top."

"Where on it?"

"Right in front. Eight inches from the end," she said. "You can see where it used to be."

I couldn't.

"It was small?"

"About three inches."

"And it disappeared after a visit?"

"Yes."

"Don't take offense, Mrs. Dewinter, but without turning around, can you tell me what's on the third shelf behind you by the mirror, sixteen inches from the left, fourth row deep, one before the last row and the wall?"

She pinched up her face. "A Navajo kachina doll Verne and I picked up in Monument Valley, Arizona, in 1983. Spring. It cost twenty-six dollars and was the second most expensive thing we brought home from that trip, the first being a blanket hanging in the study behind Verne's old desk. Would you like to see it?"

"No, I'm good." I stood up and walked to the shelf and tried to remember my instructions. I'd asked it on a bluff. There was a kachina doll on a shelf behind her. I'd have to give her that one.

"So did they know the Lladró was valuable?"

"I mentioned it was."

"You said it was worth hundreds?"

"Priceless. I mentioned it was valuable in money but then went rhapsodic on how my mother had given it to me as an engagement gift. I said it meant a lot to me."

"You think it was taken to hurt your feelings?"

Amelia nodded. "If those little shits took it, yes. If it was Verne, he's trying to tell me something."

"Like what?"

"Like it's time to let go."

Charlie sighed.

"Do your grandchildren benefit from your death?"

"Yes," she said. "They get all this." She gestured around.

The house was an old rambler, built before McMansions. Small. Nancy would be able to guesstimate its size within a square inch, but to me, it was 1950s small. The stuff on the shelves would be a nightmare to get rid of if someone wanted to make money off it. The house, however, small and dated as it was, was in a good neighborhood. Gentrification, proximity to town, and mature trees made it valuable. High six figures.

"You see," said Charlie, "The value of the stolen things are not monetary but personal. It's a murder attempt. They're trying to break Amelia's heart. Kill her from the inside."

"The murder weapon is missing kitsch, I mean, stolen heirlooms?"

He nodded. Mrs. Dewinter sighed.

"You said things. What else was taken?"

"After the missing Lladró, there was a thimble I mentioned having purchased on my honeymoon. It disappeared. Then there was the Niagara Falls souvenir spoon from the kitchen rack."

"How often do they visit?"

"Every second Sunday."

"So they were just here?"

"Yes," she said. "And that time, I laid a trap."

"What did you do?"

"I went to the dollar store and bought a tin ashtray from China. A total piece of junk."

I kept my eyes on her rather than admiring the shelves of knickknacks.

"Charlie wrote '1876' on it with a nail."

He nodded.

"Then I mentioned to the kids that it was from the 1876 Philadelphia Expo and was very valuable."

"And they took it?"

"It's gone, I think."

"You think?"

"Well, I put it down somewhere, and now I can't find it."

"So it could just be lost?"

"It could be, but not the other things. Those things I knew where to find them. The dumb ashtray was a new thing and hadn't imprinted on me yet."

"Imprinted?"

"It's a word," she said.

"Yes. Yes it is."

"It was taken," said Charlie. "Amelia said it was her most valuable thing from her great-grandfather who worked at the expo selling cigarettes, which were new then."

"So you backed it up with a story? Well done."

"Thank you," said Amelia. "Now find out which one of those louts took it and we'll prove to at least one of my granddaughters that she married a creep."

"What if they didn't do it?"

"Then I'll be seeing Verne again very soon."

CHAPTER THREE

Charlie showed me a replica of the tin ashtray that was missing. It even had the 1876 etched into it. It looked like a total piece of junk. I had to wonder how anyone could mistake this for a valuable object of any kind. Then I remembered my terrarium.

Mrs. Dewinter gave me contact information for her granddaughters and agreed to pay my rate, which I tried to discount because she was a neighbor, but she refused. I mentioned there would be expenses, and she was fine with that.

"I can afford it," she said.

I balked. It smelled like a marital case, and those are icky. The case's main selling point for me was as a way to ignore my own problems while solving someone else's. I liked that. It made me sound like a hero, a selfless superman with a magnifying glass and love of helping. There it was, a pull into action; the push, my inability to face my own problems, vis-à-vis, my own knickknack hobby obsession disaster. The world was in familiar form.

But then there was Charlie, my postman. If I screwed the case up, he could punish me with box-bursting junk mail overflow Monday through Saturday. I envisioned mounds of yard care service postcards, real estate fliers, credit card offers, savings books, time share opportunities, tire rotation deals, pizza coupons, buy-one-get-one-free cactus blowout extravaganza notice—one week only, all overflowing my recycling bin after a just short visit to my cracked and sore mailbox.

In the end, old habits took the day and I took the case. "Dear Resident" debris be damned. The life of detective is full of danger.

Mrs. Dewinter thanked me with a kiss, asked me to call her Amelia, and sent me home with a Popsicle.

Charlie drove me back and wished me good luck before disappearing into the snowy morning in his little white truck.

Inside, I surveyed my stuff, cringed, and closed the door to the basement like I was sealing a crypt.

I looked over the note Mrs. Dewinter had given me. Eliza and Hydyn Hunsing—only in Utah would parents set their son out into the world with a name spelled like that—and Jennifer and Eddie Chakmansen. The Chakmansens were closer, at least psychologically. They lived in the Salt Lake Valley, in a place called White City, a minuscule residual enclave of less than one square mile in the south end of things. It has an attitude. It is surrounded by another city called Sandy, a big suburb with clout and their own policemen. White City has, I think, its own snow shovel, but don't quote me. The place always struck me as some kind of Confederate throwback, ardently refusing to join with their neighbors for reasons of social purity or street widths. Most people in the valley know the area, but we don't talk about it because everybody needs its weirdos, and in Utah the competition is stiff, so why give them any press.

The Hunsings lived in Bountiful, a city just north of Salt Lake City in Davis County. Distance-wise, their home was probably closer to mine in Sugar House, but there was a wasteland of petroleum refineries, rail yards, and gravel pits that separated the two places. South we had a gravel pit sentry as well, keeping Salt Lake and Utah counties from cross contamination. Both Davis and Utah Counties have a reputation of being conservative. Salt Lake County has a reputation of not being as conservative but still being conservative. This is Utah. In Salt Lake City, you can dance on Sunday, have fewer than fifteen kids, and show your shoulders. Like I said, there was a psychological prejudice against anyone outside of the Salt Lake valley. I'm sure it went the other way, too, but I don't get to those other places much to check. I just assume they're all freaks.

Shoveling my walks would wait another day. They'd already survived a week, What was the hurry now? Spring was around the corner. I got into my little green Prius and set out for the southland.

It was a weekday, around noon, so the traffic was light. People wouldn't be home. Nine-to-five jobs made it easy for disreputable people like me to case joints. There's a thin line between detective and burglar, I'm told, but I've never seen it.

The house was a pale boxy split-entry. Split-entries are an architect's way of telling wheelchair users to fuck off. Door opens to a five-foot square landing with immediate stairs up or down, usually too narrow. They are a real low point in house design. White City had a lot of them.

The Chakmansens used the same snow removal service as I did. None. I saw tire tracks leading in and out of the connected two-car garage a few times, all on the left side. No one had stepped on their sidewalk or approached the front door. The snow was pristine there, about a week old. Dry and crunchy. It was garbage day. The wheels of the big can led behind the garage door.

I think there's some law about when garbage ceases to be your property and becomes available for searching. You'd think I'd know it. It could have been a question on my private eye license exam, but it wasn't. They didn't even offer a little cartoon booklet like the DMV that would show me in bright easy-to-read pictures how far from a suspect I should follow, or the correct way to peek between blinds. I'd had to wing it. There wasn't even a practical test where I had to smoke cigarettes under a bright spotlight or get pistol-whipped climbing into a trailer. Such disappointment.

The road was public, so I figured the garbage cans were, too. I parked in front of the house, looked up and down the quiet street, and tiped the can over. Out spilled garbage. They liked Mountain Dew and cut-rate bottled marinara sauce. They didn't recycle. They'd forgotten their broccoli until it had liquefied and had a cat. Maybe two. They'd cleaned the litter box that week. Who said being a private investigator wasn't glamorous?

I saw some papers stuck to the bottom and crawled in after them. I figured them to be more useful than cat feces. I refused to think of the rubbish as refuse. Clues, dammit, clues! My nose would recover. I didn't like this shirt much. There in back, sticking to the plastic walls in six places, I peeled credit card statements out of a glue-puddle of Taco Bell Fire sauce and turned butternut squash that apropos to its name squished between my knuckles.

It was because I was inside the plastic nightmare of suburban waste that I didn't hear the car pull up behind me. When it honked, however, echoing off the walls and into my spin like a piece of rebar on the freeway, I exhaled my held breath and sucked in deep the tainted fragrance that now included chili with onions and used foot powder.

I backed out slowly, trying to think of what to say, some excuse for what I was doing. Dropped my cellphone in their garbage? Heard a raccoon and wanted to get rabies for the insurance payout? But all I could do was wonder if my clothes would burn or if they'd need to be buried in the desert super-fund site.

"What are you doing?" It was the obvious question. I should have seen it coming.

I got up, straightened myself to standing like I belonged there, and said, "This is none of your business."

"I live here," she said. It was a woman. She was in little white Corolla. She had to be Jennifer. Mrs. Dewinter's granddaughter.

"Do you live here?" I said, buying time to think. I smelled my clothes and wondered if there was still a county web page listing the days when it's okay to burn things.

"Yes. That's why I want to know why you're in my garbage," she said.

"Are you the homeowner?" Maybe if I kept asking the same question in different ways, something good would happen.

"Yes. I own it with my husband."

"Oh, well, I'll need to talk to both of you. When will you both be home? I'll make an appointment and explain everything then."

"He's inside now."

"And he lives here too?" Smooth, Tony. Smooth.

"Who are you?"

"Me? Oh, I'm Max Garlicscent." It was the first thing that popped into my mind.

"Do I need to call the police, Max?"

"What? No. I have a great proposal for you and your husband, Eddie."

"How do you know my husband's name?"

The answer was "your grandmother told me." Another possible truth would be "I saw it on the sticky papers I'd stuffed into my pocket." Neither one would help me.

"I've done research. You're the perfect household for what I have to propose."

"You want to propose something about our garbage?"

I smiled. Nodded slowly. Paused. "Yes," I said, drawing out the word. "Yes. That is exactly why I'm here."

"Is there money involved?"

"You'll make money."

"How?"

"It's complicated. I'll make an appointment."

"We can make money? Well, Eddie's inside and I have an hour before I have to go to my next job. Now works."

"Swell."

She pushed a button on her visor and the garage door rolled up. There was room for only one car. The other side of the garage was filled with storage shelves, boxes, bags, unused snow-blower. It looked like mine.

She drove in and stopped, waiting for me to follow.

"Let me just get this," I said and pushed the garbage back inside and righted the can. "I'll just freshen up."

Jenni waited for me. She watched suspiciously, which meant she had brain cells in operation. I went to my car, stuck the stolen papers under my seat, and then stood up and made a big production of wiping my hands with a wet wipe I'd grabbed from a barbecue place last year. "There. All tidy."

I skated up the icy driveway until I was in the garage with her. "Sure you don't want to make an appointment?"

"No."

"No? No, you're not sure?"

"No. We're doing this now."

"Good. That's the kind of enthusiasm that'll make this work."

I followed her in. I couldn't tell if she'd bought into my lie or was playing me. I'm usually a good liar, but my material stank that day. I had a feeling I was about to be used for something.

"Eddie, someone here to see you."

"Both of you," I said.

"Both of us," she called.

The house was neater than mine and less cluttered than Mrs. Dewinter's, both statements saying precious little. It looked like just the two of them lived there. No sign of kids. The living room where she began to lead me was done in a modest older style of plaid-patterned couch that didn't get a lot of use. Smelling me, Jenni changed her mind and led me instead, not to the kitchen, which might be hosed off after I left or back to the garage for the same reason, but down a main hall. I saw an open door and an unmade bed at the far end. There was a bathroom to the left with hand towels I knew enough never to use, and a man cave to the right.

Before I got a place all to myself that became a man-house, I'd had a man cave not unlike this one. I'd actually had several rooms, but one of them had been a lot like this with a computer, a top-of-the line gaming chair, double monitors, game controllers, fans, and rocking headphones. The man I assumed to be Eddie hadn't noticed us come in. He was playing a first-person shooting game I wasn't immediately familiar with. I'd been out of gaming for several days and had lost touch. He swerved right, dodged left, and strafed back. He was in a helicopter.

"Eddie," said his wife.

Nothing.

"Eddie," she said a little louder.

An alert in red flashed on the screen, "Nowhere to run!" The avatar turned to face attackers waiting for him in the back seats. He said, and here I mean Eddie speaking in real words, not internet chat, "See you in hell!" His character produced a club, bashed out the helicopter window and leaped out.

"Eddie!" screamed his wife.

He jumped. This time out of his chair, not the helicopter. That had already happened.

He turned around to face us. She stepped forward and turned off the computer. Not the monitor. The computer. Game over.

"Don't sneak up on me," he said, and then to me, "Who are you?"

"This man is out making money today," said Jenni. "That's right. He's working. On a job. A job I bet he hates because he has to dig through garbage for it. And yet, a job he does because I bet he has responsibilities that are more important to him than a little inconvenience and loss of me-time."

Yep, I was being used.

CHAPTER FOUR

"You smell like it," said Eddie after taking a sniff.

"He smells like an adult?" asked Jenni.

He scowled at her but then averted his eyes. "No, he smells like he was in a garbage can."

"I could make an appointment and come back," I said, hoping to make that dodge finally work.

No soap.

"Sit down. We'll talk here." She kicked a stack of gaming magazines onto the floor. I'd subscribed to many of them and probably had a box of back issues in my basement. The keep pile.

"He can't sit down like that," said Eddie. "The smell."

"I doubt he can cut through what's already here." She sat down and patted the seat next to her for me.

I don't know if there was a smell in the room. I couldn't tell. Not in my state. But there probably was. I saw a bevy of Hot Pocket wrappers in an overflowing garbage can and a rigid brown gym sock under the table.

Jenni's eyes pierced me, and I sat down.

"Excellent," I said. "Again, like I said, you guys are just the demographic we're looking for. Your taste of smell is perfect."

"Taste of smell?" he said.

"Yes. Exactly."

They both stared—he at me, confused; she with venom behind her lashes at him.

I scanned the room, looking for a little tin ashtray that would make this whole shit show worthwhile.

No soap.

"Well?" said Eddie.

"Are you hiring?" asked Jenni.

Eddie blushed.

"Yes."

"Yes?"

"Yes."

"And?" said Eddie.

"The future," I said. "Think about it."

"Okay …" he said.

"It's where all of us are going to spend the rest of our lives." I prayed they weren't Ed Wood fans.

Jenni said, "Isn't that from Plan 9 From Outerspace?"

No soap.

"Yes. Ed Wood was a visionary. That's why I'm here."

Jenni's expression turned back to me. It was time to say something.

"You guys are what? Mid-thirties?"

"We're both twenty-six," Eddie said.

"Perfect."

"Mr. Garlicscent, can you come to the point?"

"That's your name?"

Did I really call myself that? Shit. I guess I had.

"Call me Max."

"You were born with that name?" asked Jenni. She was on to me.

"No, I chose it when I started Home Composting Company Corporation Limited."

"Home Composting …"

"Company Corporation Limited," I supplied, hoping I wouldn't forget the name in five minutes. Please, God, no squirrels.

"I can tell by the quality of your garbage, full of organic matter and biodegradables, detritus, and intrituses, that you'd qualify to be one of our test homes to demonstrate to the city that home composting is not only affordable but fun."

"You mentioned money," said Jenni. "You remember money, don't you, Eddie? That thing we used to have?"

Ouch.

He wouldn't look at her.

"Yes. My research has determined that high-quality compost

22

like you are making already, with just a few worms and some time, could be worth up to five hundred dollars a ton."

"A ton?"

"That's really not much," I said. "A cubic Varconium in shop talk. About the size of a sandbox."

Let me say right here, that I was new to the detective thing. My olfactory senses were overwhelmed, my brain was short-circuiting because of the marital tension in the room, which was as palpable as the peanut butter on my elbows. I prayed no one would call me on the made-up word.

"Varconium?"

No soap.

"Yes. We add varcomelite, my own invention, to the mixture to create super earthworms that turn the soil into a powerhouse of growing potential. A powerhouse of growing potential."

"How big do the worms get?"

"Just over three feet."

They stared.

"After years in the project," I added. "I have an old swimming pool where I grow them. In such a space they can grow large. In your backyard, I doubt they'd be bigger than a foot. And they probably wouldn't bite."

There. My senses were coming back. I was cleverly planning my exit. Nothing gets you out of a sticky situation quite like someone wanting—no NEEDING—to get rid of you.

"Is there work involved?" asked Jenni. "Maybe something to get someone out of the house once in a goddamn month?"

"Yes, the manure fields need raking."

"Manure field?" said Eddie.

"Yes, for the varcomelite to really work, we need to add night soil to the mix."

"That's shit, Eddie," said Jenni. "You'll have to shit outside again."

"You're kidding," he said.

"Do I smell like I'm kidding?"

They had no answer.

"Do either of you smoke?"

"Is that a problem?"

"I'll need to balance the 4H factor if you do. I thought I saw an ashtray."

"We don't smoke."

"I could have sworn I saw a little silver ashtray," said I, ever so cleverly.

"I'll need to get paid sooner than later," said Eddie. "Is there a signing bonus?"

"And we don't have to buy anything from you?" said Jenni.

"Not if you get three of your neighbors to sign up."

"There it is," said Eddie. "I won't do an MLM."

"You'll do something, you loaf," said Jenni. "I'm here busting my ass working not one, not two, but three jobs while you're here finding yourself on the Planet Mayhem."

I knew Planet Mayhem. The powerups were awesome.

"And it's not enough that you don't bring money into the house, you cost us."

"It's just as expensive to live alone as with two."

"Have we forgotten about last November's Candy Crush bill?"

He looked ashamed, turned his face and mumbled, "I deleted that one."

"Eddie Chakmansen, you will face your responsibilities to this family if it means crawling around in garbage cans and shitting on the lawn like a real man."

I was a real man. Cool.

"I can see you have a lot to discuss." I stood up.

"Sit down, Garlicstench."

I didn't think that was the name I'd used before, but hell if I could remember it was. I sat down.

"Eddie?" said Jenni.

"What?"

"Eddie, opportunity has actually come knocking. Or rather ferreting through your used tissue."

Ouch.

Ick.

"Are you going to welcome your new partner?"

"I have to finish my album," he whispered. "It's close."

"It's been close since you were in seventh grade," said Jenni. "Just as soon as you get an instrument, remember? And learn to play it."

As much as the situation stank, and as awkward as it was, it was better than my last marital case. Then, both parties accused the other of being shitty. This one-sided barrage was a relief.

"And the worms can be used for meat," I said from some terrible dungeon in my mind, "thus shrinking your grocery bill."

They both looked at me like I'd asked them to eat worms.

"How many hours a day are we talking?" asked Eddie.

"We're talking hours per week," I said. "After startup, it won't be more than ten hours a week. Less if you take corn out of your diet."

"Signing bonus?"

"I'll tell you what," I said. "I'll talk to my people and get back to you on this. Maybe you can recruit members of your family."

"I'd rather shovel shit than do multi-level-marketing," Eddie said.

"Why not do both?" I said.

"Eddie?" said Jenni. "If there's not money coming in this week, you're a composter. Understand?"

"Excellent," I said. "Eddie, Jenni, glad to have you aboard."

Eddie shook my hand and regretted it. The mayonnaise between my fingers had thawed since outside. Jenni just nodded.

Before they could ask for contact information or schedule an appointment—now they'd want one—I was out the door. I made fresh fast footprints across their walk, lawn, and rose bushes before I jumped into my car and sped away.

Driving home on the freeway with the windows rolled down, my face turning blue from the cold, I wondered what I'd accomplished by my visit. The dumpster dive was par for the course in detective work. The rest, well, that was all to keep them from calling the police on me for being on par. That was one topic the detective license bureau made sure you knew. Don't cross the cops. If there was a lesson every cop felt qualified to teach, especially to people getting paid more than them, getting away with more crimes than they were (sometimes) and usually smelling better, it was that one. How they envied me, my frostbitten nose, ruined clothes, and fragrant car.

I took the exit toward home when traffic came to a complete stop. Lucky for me, I was paying attention or my Prius would have been a bumper sticker on a snowplow. Somebody had spun and crashed into the separating barrier, tagging a half dozen cars as he did.

I put my car in park and rolled up the window. A couple warm breaths and that was enough. Better frozen than that smell.

I dug the stolen papers out from under my seat and read them.

They were three credit cards bills. One of them new, with a transferred balance of three thousand six hundred dollars. The others all listed small transactions, a dollar or two at a time, sometimes five or six per day. They added up. I recognized the names of software companies, the really shitty ones with micro transactions in them. There was Planet Mayhem. He'd bought five powerup boxes within five minutes. I guess Eddie had a real hard level. Totaling all the bills, the number was approaching ten thousand dollars. All the bills were dated this month.

Jenni was going to shit when she found out. At least I'd given Eddie an idea of what to do when that happened.

Rake it into compost, for you readers slow on the callback.

The traffic moved. I moved with it.

A cop had appeared and moved the crashes to the shoulder while it was sorted out.

I crawled by at the requisite five-miles-per-hour-gawker-speed and didn't see anyone hurt. A lot of dents, broken lights, and a wet spot around one guy's crotch was the extent of it.

Back home, I left the windows open to air out my car. I doubted the cold, still air in my garage would do anything, so I coated my seat in Febreze before going in. The world smelled like daffodils in a landfill.

I stripped out of my clothes in the garage, then crab-walked through the house for fear of working any molecules deeper into my skin, giving me subcutaneous stink sores for years. Past boxes that mocked me and trash that swooned, I made my way to the shower. I turned on the water, felt it get hot, and slithered in.

Time to get clean.

But alas.

No soap.

CHAPTER FIVE

Eddie was under the gun, and Jenni had a point to point it at him. I'd mucked up the meeting but still called it progress. Mrs. Dewinter's theory of attempted murder by shoplifting seemed far-fetched to me. If you want to kill someone, stuffing your pockets with marbles didn't seem like a good method. Stealing stuff to pawn to pay micro transactions so your wife won't find out and mount your balls over the fireplace—that made more sense to me. Been there, done that. Attempted murder is rare. Murder itself even more so, if you think about it. Flaner's Razor: 'Don't ascribe to murder that which can be adequately explained by dipshitness.' Okay, I gotta work on that. Wikipedia has standards.

Nevertheless, here was motive, means, and opportunity. I almost called Amelia right then, crowing about my success when I got out of the shower. Shower thoughts can stray. Luckily, I hesitated. I didn't know how much to charge the expense report for my clothes. Would I need to get the Prius detailed?

Also, I hadn't checked out the other suspect. And I had absolutely no proof. That's always a problem. If one doesn't use evidence for conclusions, what are they? An American. But I would rise above that, and I would find out how much a new pair of pants costs and if I needed new upholstery. Might as well check out what Eliza and Hydyn were up to while I was doing that. Maybe I'd find some evidence if I looked. You know, just to be different.

By the way, shampoo isn't just for hair.

In clean underwear and a stolen bathrobe smelling of Herbal Essence, I removed some of the trash from my general living areas. I got the idea from the garbage can. I put my garbage in one of those, and my place looked much better. What to do with the tole-painting supplies and obsidian shards would have to wait for another day. I couldn't remember why I'd brought them upstairs. Or when.

My doorbell rang.

"Who is it?"

"It's us, Flaner. Let us in." It was the voice of Standard Flox. One of the gang.

"Why?"

"Because it's fucking cold out here!" And Dara Sutter.

"You know it's common courtesy to shovel your walks, right?" Garrett Corda.

"Only if you want people to come to your door," said Critter, Garrett's alter ego and comedy partner. A puppet.

"Is Perry there too?"

"Fucking let us in!"

"He's driving around the block looking for a parking place," said Garrett.

"Why? What's wrong with out front or my driveway?"

"Too obvious, he says," explained Standard. "People could be following us."

"Flaner, if you don't let us in, I will put my foot so far up your ass, your breath will smell like athlete's foot."

Dara has a way of saying things and convinced me. I opened the door.

In came the gang, all semi-pro (read amateur) comedians who I hang out with, usually at The Comedy Cellar club downtown. Perry, Perry Whitehouse, I'd call an up-and-coming comedian since he's really good, and his career actually pays money. He's nuts though. Crazy, as in 'needs medication or he'll circle the block for hours waiting for the spooks to get tired of following him and then change his name for a few weeks in case they changed their minds.' I noticed him jogging—no—running up the street and through the door. He barreled into Standard, blindsiding him and sending him over the couch.

"Hi, Perry," I said.

Lying flat on his chest, he kicked the door shut. "Hi, Tony."

"What the hell, Perry?" said Standard.

"Sorry, Stan. Had to keep up the momentum."

Standard liked to be called Stan. I called him Standard because that's how the mechanisms worked between us.

Critter, the googly-eyed felt-fanged puppet on Garrett's arm, surveyed the room. "How long does it take to move in?"

"A while," said I.

"Just getting up?" said Dara looking at my ensemble. "You're really letting yourself go."

"I was working a case. And it got … uh, dirty."

"You're still doing that?" said Standard. "I thought you'd have given that up by now."

"Not yet."

"Pay up," said Dara.

Standard dug a ten-dollar bill out of his pocket and gave it to her.

"Thanks for believing in me," I said.

"It was an easy over-under. I might still have to pay Critter. You think you'll still be doing the detective thing next week?"

"Yes."

"Pay up," said the puppet.

"Next week I will. If he lasts."

"Great to have you guys behind me," I said.

"I believe in you," said Perry, closing the blinds.

"Thanks."

"I think you'll make it to Valentine's Day."

I can't blame my friends. They've seen me pinball between jobs and hobbies like, well … a pinball. Nothing lasts more than a few months. Seven, according to data analysis. I get bored and move on. When things get tough, I get going. Not as in "to get the tough things done," but get going to do something else that's not so tough. I've made progress in this area, thanks to my new career as a private detective. I learned how good it feels to finally finish something. Success is cool. Who knew?

"Why are you here?" I asked.

"Not glad to see us?" asked Dara. She fluttered her eyelashes. She was a cute girl. Very short. She reminded people of an elf until she opened her mouth and placed her origin nearer a fishing boat than Rivendell.

"Sure," I said. "Why are you here?"

"This town is dead. There's nothing to do," said Standard.

"Entertain us," said Critter.

"Don't be so blunt," said Garrett to his hand.

"Really? You came here because you're bored?"

"You got any booze?"

"Maybe."

"I'll get it," said Perry and disappeared into the kitchen. Of all my friends, he'd visited me the most. He'd even helped me unpack a box. A box.

Standard went for the easy chair but backed off when Dara gave him a look. She took that, he retreated to the sofa with Garrett and Critter.

"Vodka or bourbon?" called Perry. "Oh, and peppermint schnapps."

"Vodka." Dara.

"Bourbon." Standard.

"Nothing for me, unless there's a Coke." Garrett.

"Peppermint schnapps in a tall glass." Critter.

"Tony?" said Perry.

"Bourbon."

"You got Cokes?"

"Did you look in the fridge?"

"No."

"Try there."

Dara turned on the television, and I dove to the DVD player before it could activate it.

"Old home movies," I said. "Nothing you'd be interested in."

"Uh-huh."

"Get with it, Tony," said Standard. "The internet has all the smut now."

"I don't know what you're talking about." I slid the disk into a blank case. "Firefly?"

"Got anything good?" said Critter.

We all turned and stared at him. Including Garrett. "What?" said the puppet. "It's overrated."

"Shut him up, Garrett, or he's going into the shredder."

"You've never even seen it," said Garrett.

"Oh, and you have?" Critter said.

"Twice. I own it."

"Where was I?"

"Don't ask me."

Did I say that Perry is insane? I meant to say, he's the most insane, the one who's been diagnosed and medicated. All my friends are nuts. Like attracts like. I'm the only sane one.

Perry came out with punch bowl full of ice, arms full of bottles, hands full of mixers, and red Solo cups in his teeth. I helped him put it all on the freshly cleared coffee table.

"A flash party?" I said.

"That's as good a name as anything," said Garrett, holding his stare at Critter.

Standard said, maybe to calm the mood between the two, "There is nothing to do in this town in January. After the holidays, everyone holes up. Barry barely makes an effort at the Cellar. He's on vacation. Someplace warm and smog free."

"So with Barry gone, we don't get the one complimentary pitcher of beer anymore?" I asked.

"Thus the flash party."

I poured drinks with Perry. He took straight vodka but measured his dose. Five bottle caps. I poured coke into my bourbon and set a tall schnapps in front of the puppet. I waited for him to taste it.

"I'm letting it breathe," he said.

Perry found a duct-taped bean-bag chair I've been meaning to re-upholster, maybe in burlap, and flopped down as Dara turned off the TV.

"It's the holiday let-down," said Perry after a sip, grimace, and sip. "American society is amped on consumerism all through the holidays. From Halloween through New Year, it's spend spend spend. This is the hangover period when the useless crap we went into debt for doesn't fill the fundamental psychological yearning for meaning and happiness."

He made a lot of sense. He does that sometimes, a lot, actually.

"Now is the time to get out and enjoy the season," said Critter, still not drinking his schnapps.

"Buying season?" said Standard. "Perry just—"

"No, you ignoramus," said the puppet. "The winter season. There is an actual season outside. Globally recognized with unique characteristics. It's called winter, and it has a beauty all its own."

"You doing a lot of bobsledding this year, Critter?" said Dara. "Cross country? Skating?"

"I can't get anyone to take me." He turned to look at Garrett.

"Winter sucks," said Garrett. "Winter sports are all echoes of desperate means our ancestors invented so as not to die in this wonderful season called winter. It blows."

"Are all gifts meaningless?" I asked. "Can't some of them carry certain emotional power, or get it, and thus justify its existence?"

Perry wrinkled his brow, either to ponder my question or to endure the vodka.

Garrett and Critter stared at each other maliciously. Opposite sides of the winter debate. Critter was in a confrontational mood. Garrett almost never was. It was strange to see them both on that wavelength.

Dara closed her eyes and drank as if feeling the alcohol heat her veins. She was in my chair.

Standard tried to drink his bourbon straight but was now, as causally as he could, adding Coke to his cup.

"Sentimental value?" said Perry. "Personal value outside the material worth?"

"Exactly."

"That can happen, but it's a primitive emotion. Smacks of talismanic magic."

"Are we going to get a fucking occult lecture now?"

"Do you want one?"

"No." It was unanimous.

"The problem lies in placing real emotional energy into a material thing."

"You're walking the line, Perry," said Dara. I'd not heard Perry's occult lecture, but apparently they had and didn't want to again.

"The danger is in losing the thing. It's a thing and thus can be lost."

"Or broken," said Standard.

"Burned," said Dara without opening her eyes.

"Stolen?" said I.

"Right," said Perry. "The loss is huge. All materialism threatens this, but when you imprint upon an object, you're setting yourself up for the worst. Also, it can lead to hoarding, a sure sign of mental instability."

"Now you'll say that photo albums are a fetish," said Dara.

"I won't take it that far," said Perry.

"You would if you weren't in range of my drink."

Perry didn't answer that.

"To each his own," said Standard pouring himself another bourbon and Coke. "If you want stuff, you should have stuff."

"Go environment," said Critter.

"I mean, if Tony wants to keep things that mean something to him, why shouldn't he be allowed?"

"So this is about Tony?" said Dara.

"Cost of the room."

"Do you own a storage unit?" asked Perry. "That, in my opinion is where the line is."

"I do not," I said.

"You are safe."

"And the surprising fact that we can actually walk through your house without tripping on everything is a good sign. You're a slob, not a nut."

"What about souvenirs?" I asked.

"What? Like Garrett's button collection?"

"It's valuable."

"The fuck it is. You don't even sew."

"They're to look at."

"You have a whole shelf of them."

"It's my shelf and I like to look at them," Garrett said. "They bring back memories."

"State memory," said Perry. "A lot of work has been done on that. That's one way this all makes sense."

"Here he goes again," said Standard, "going off on the state."

"Shut your hole, you moron," said the puppet. "He's not talking politics."

"Mind your friend, Garrett, or I'll punch him."

"He's right, Critter," said Garrett. "You're being an asshole tonight. Maybe you've had enough to drink."

The puppet lowered his head in shame.

"State memory is a kind of memory trigger. Being in an emotional state will bring on certain memories associated with it. And vice versa."

"Why not call it associated memory then?" asked Garrett.

"Because he has the state on his mind," said Standard.

"Just because you're not interested in politics doesn't mean politics isn't interested in you."

"So a statue," I continued, "say, received at Christmas, could act as an associated trigger to recall feelings from those times?"

"Yep."

"So what's the harm?"

"I told you the harm. It can go too far."

"Seems to me," said Dara, still not opening her eyes but draining her cup, "that keeping shit is like an old-fashioned hard drive."

"What?"

"You know, where you store your pictures and projects."

"But it's a thing."

"Okay, then like a fucking three-dimensional photo album. You dicks happy now?" Dara held her cup out and jiggled it. "More, please."

I poured her another and put it in her outstretched hand. Her eyes were still shut. Critter still hadn't touched his drink.

"Remember, Tony," said Perry as he poured out five more capfuls of Smirnoff. "It's okay to own things, just don't let them own you."

"Firefly?" I said. "Whenever someone space-swears, we drink."

Critter sighed but acquiesced.

I found the discs, put them in, and, still in my robe and undies, settled in with my friends for a night of binge watching and binge drinking.

It was a great gorram night.

CHAPTER SIX

I told myself that I slept late the next day to let the traffic patterns ease for my planned trip to Bountiful. It had nothing to do with my hangover, which was bad. When we ran out of bourbon and vodka we drank peppermint schnapps. Even Critter's cup was empty before the party ended.

Perry stopped drinking in time to chauffeur everyone home before dawn, and I painted my pillow with drool until two o'clock in the afternoon, when I figured the roads would be adequately deserted.

They were. It was a weekday and mid-afternoon, and the responsible people of Utah were working or doing their responsible things, and I had an easy drive to Bountiful. On the way, I chewed aspirin like they were Juicy Fruit and slammed Gatorade like it didn't taste like diluted horse piss.

Bountiful is a quiet town. I almost never hear about serious crimes there. That to me says it's probably a really boring place, but, like I said, I never go there. Freaks.

I left the freeway and wove through suburban streets until I found the house.

It was nice. Much nicer than Jenni and Eddie's. No split-entry here—something built this century when river stone and stucco were in abundance.

There were no garbage cans set in front of the house, and part of me rejoiced. I saw lights on inside. Then I saw a face pressed to glass staring at me in my parked car staring at them. I'd been busted again.

I got out and headed up to the door with a spring in my step and a smile on my face as I wondered if the compost shtick would work here. The walks had been shoveled. And salted. Garden lights turned on when they sensed me passing. The composting story was out. These people already had their shit together.

I rang the bell.

The garage door opened.

The door opened.

A woman stood in the doorway. Mascara streaked black lines from her red eyes down her pale cheeks, but she looked at me with piercing strength and a firm chin. Chins can look if they want to.

"Hi, I'm a friend of your sister Jenni's, and she—"

A Volvo backed out of the garage. It squealed on the pavement and then sped off, the garage door closing softly behind it.

"You're a friend of Jenni's?"

"Yes."

"Will you be a friend of mine?" she asked.

"You're Eliza?"

"Yes."

"Sure."

"Follow that car."

She grabbed me by the hand and led me back to my Prius. She was wearing casual slacks and a blouse. The kind of thing you go shopping in but not to dinner. More than hang around the house, less than an interview with the queen. She had no jacket.

"I'm Mr. Um ..." I tried to remember the name I'd given Jenni. "Stinky Joe."

"Follow him."

"He's got a head start."

"You've got a gas pedal. Go."

Another goddamned domestic case.

I sighed but followed the car.

"You could have followed him in your Tahoe. I saw it in your garage."

"I've been drinking," she said. "And crying."

"Why are you crying?"

"None of your business."

"I'll just let you off at the mission," I said.

"No. Follow him."

"Is he going to another woman?" I said.

"I hope so."

"What?"

"I hope it's another woman. But I think it's worse."

"What do you think it is?"

"We'll see."

"Will we?"

"I'll give you a thousand dollars to follow him."

"Where is he going?"

"He's turning onto the freeway," she said.

"And after that?"

"We'll see."

"Let me see your checkbook."

"Don't you trust me? Jenni will vouch for me."

I played a hunch. "No, she won't."

She looked hurt. "Okay. Here. She took the wedding ring off her finger and put it into my hand. It was big. Lots of diamonds. Lots of big diamonds.

"Hold that until I give you the money, okay?"

"What's going on, Eliza?"

"Just follow him."

"I am."

She opened my glove compartment and took out the butterscotch candies I kept there and started eating them.

I followed the Volvo onto I-80 West.

"You and Hydyn having problems?"

She ignored the question.

"Jenni and Eddie are on the rocks, too," I said.

"Different reasons."

"Eddie's a slacker, Hydyn's a…"

"Who are you?" she said.

"Uhm, I'm… do you believe in composting?"

She opened my glove box again and pulled out my car registration.

"Tony Flaner," she said. "Sugar House."

"Yes, I deal in shit."

"You're a cop or something. I read about you. Something in

Thailand."

"A private investigator," I said. "Like I told you, I deal in shit."

We passed the airport exit and headed toward the salt flats. The taillights of the classic car were unmistakable on the freeway. The sun was going down.

"A thousand dollars buys consultation services," I said. "What's up? I actually have a bit of experience in this kind of thing."

"What kind of thing?"

"Marital meltdowns, cheating, divorce, screaming, custody battles of CD collections."

"Don't make assumptions."

"Then tell me." I felt strangely in control, like Tom Selleck in an Hawaiian Ferrari, mustached and macho. It didn't last.

We rounded the tip of Tooele, the last bastion of civilization between Zion, Utah, and Wendover, Nevada.

"We're going to Wendover?"

She started to cry.

The road went nowhere else. On one end of I-80 from the valley was Evanston, Wyoming, home of beer kegs and cheap liquor. On the other was Wendover, Nevada, the closest place to Salt Lake City to throw your money away on green felt tables. There was more beyond Wendover, like Donner Pass, but for our purposes, I knew we were going to the cut-rate Vegas border town loaded with cheap drinks, cheap hotels, and cheap women.

Eliza cried for an hour—softly, thank God, or I'd have pulled over and watched starlight on the salt flats rather than continue in that emotionally compromised condition. A man is weak to a woman's crying. I saw it on Star Trek. A lady's tears ruins a man's ability to command Constellation-class starships, unless they're in love with their ships, which is kinda creepy. Kirk knows all about this. I wasn't sure I loved my Prius that much, so I was glad she bottled most of it up.

"Why do you stay with him," I asked, "if he makes you this miserable?"

She didn't answer. I let it lie.

We drove for a while in the dimming light. It was stark but

40

serene, desert flatland with crusty snow under a dimming sunset. She stared out the windshield. I fell into my thoughts, a quiet deep reverie, riding the road vibrations up my legs—

"Why did you come to the house?" she said suddenly, loudly, breaking the silence in a firm hard tone. I jumped and swerved into the right lane.

"I mentioned Jenni," I said when the car was straightened and my heart settled.

"My sister?"

"Do you guys get along?"

"Not really. I think she's stupid to stay married to her husband."

"Could she say the same about you?"

Her eyes went back to staring. I was almost ready a few minutes later when she spoke again. Loudly. Suddenly. I only swerved a little that time.

"You didn't answer my question," she said.

"I'm working a case."

"For whom?"

And here all those hours of watching old TV shows paid off. "I can't disclose my client. It's confidential."

"There's no law that says you can't," she said.

"Really?"

"Really."

"How do you know?"

"I'm a lawyer."

This would have been a good piece of information to have had before this moment, obvious information a detective should have had gathered at the original case interview. 'Oh, hey, Mrs. Dewinter, can you tell me anything about your kids I'll be investigating? What they're like? Their ages? Likes and dislikes? Jobs?' I'd gotten some addresses and names. In my defense, by not asking such obvious and necessary questions, I'm sure I'd left Mrs. Dewinter in a sense and wonder at my confidence. Plus I was new at this detective thing.

"What does Hydyn do?"

"He's also a lawyer," she said.

"Successful?"

"He used to be. It's why I don't practice anymore."

"Used to?"

"Not so much the last couple of years." She went back to staring.

Silence.

"So who's your client?"

I jumped out of my skin again and found the shoulder.

"What is with you?" I said. "Can't you, like, clear your throat or something before you go into command courtroom tone?"

"I don't know what you mean," she said.

"Loud voice after long silence. Stop it."

She turned back to the road.

The silence settled again. Snow glistened under starlight, cold and far. The drive would only be a couple of hours, but for many people, it'd taken lifetimes.

"It may not be the law," I said suddenly and loudly.

She let out a little shriek and jumped in her seat before turning to me, wild-eyed.

"But," I continued, "my ethics won't allow me to disclose my client."

"Okay, okay, I get it."

"About my client?"

"About startling volumes in quiet, dark confined spaces."

The Volvo sped along. My little car struggled to keep up with it.

Soon the lights of Wendover shone at the end of the road. I closed in on Hydyn's car in case he exited.

He did.

I followed him into Wendover.

Wendover, or Bend-Over as some less-than-lucky Utahns call it, exists only to serve the sinners of Salt Lake. There is no reason for it to exist where it does except that it's in Nevada, where gambling is legal and close enough for a day trip from the Wasatch Front, the name of the belt of towns under the Wasatch mountains where like eighty percent of Utah's population hangs out.

At night, Wendover is almost pretty. Neon lights sparkle and lure, distracting from the wasteland of sun-beaten trailer homes and all-night pawn shops that don't have as much neon. A liquor store the size of a suburban mall offers beer with real alcohol. Also open all night.

We followed the Volvo to the Salty Saddle Casino. He pulled into valet parking and climbed out. He had an overnight bag in the trunk. Eliza sucked in her breath as she saw him get it and go inside.

I cleared my throat. "What now?" I asked.

"Follow him."

I looked around for a parking place. Valet is not usually the Flaner way.

"Go after him. Go. Don't lose him. I'm paying you."

"But—"

"I'll stay with the car."

I looked at her, thought of my lovely green hybrid disappearing in a long-con car-jacking across state lines but then noticed her big diamond wedding ring on my pinky.

I got out. "Don't go far," I said.

"I won't go anywhere if you don't give me the keys."

"Right. Good plan." I gave her the keys.

"If you have to park, leave word where I can find you at the reception desk."

She shooed me away, her wild eyes searching behind me to where her husband had gone. I knew those eyes. I'd seen them in my last case just before the client threw my new digital camera off a six-story terrace.

CHAPTER SEVEN

This was a theft case, not a marital one. I worked for Mrs. Amelia Dewinter, searching for a missing knickknack that was probably hiding behind a thousand other knickknacks. I was not working for Eliza, following a cheating husband to a rendezvous.

Oh, wait. Yes. I was.

Shit.

I'd even said that for what she was paying, I'd give her advice. That's agreement to an oral contract, right? I should ask a lawyer. Like the one in my car.

Shit. Shit.

I saw Hydyn talking to a pit boss by a counter. They seemed like old friends. He swung a touchscreen computer around to show him, and Hydyn touched a couple buttons and turned it back. He then headed into the casino. He didn't have his bag anymore.

The casino was a casino, a little more modern than what I remembered Wendover usually offering but still a far cry from Mafia-infused glitz of real shake-down palaces. It was a corporate casino, which has got to be the epitome of the capitalist dream. The lights were full spectrum but low, the carpets the work of a fried drug addict expressing the paranoia with geometric shapes on fifty-year-old fabric.

I saw Hydyn, which is pronounced like Hayden, you know, like the real name. I watched him take a chair at one of two twenty-one tables. I did the math. 2 x 21 = 42. Forty-two, the answer to life, the universe and everything. I walked in confidently since I knew the score, which, like I said, was forty-two.

I took a seat with Hydyn and two other players, a chain-smoking woman whose laugh and cough were indistinguishable and an older old guy unwilling to admit he'd long lost the balding

44

battle and had a yard of wispy comb-over cemented to his scalp.

The pit boss from before appeared, put a tray of chips in front of Hydyn, and was tipped a yellow chip for his effort.

Hydyn stacked the chips and then put four green ones in front him.

I pulled out my wallet, found a twenty and slapped it down on the felt like I owned the place. I got one yellow chip for it.

A little plastic sign by the dealer's elbow said $20 minimum, no limit after nine o'clock. It was 9:05.

I left the chip there like I had it to lose. That was lunch for a week with taco Tuesdays.

The cards came. The smoker got a five, Hairball a queen, me an ace, Hydyn a nine, and the dealer a six.

For a while I tried to be a card counter. I didn't get very far, but I know the game. There's math involved. And concentration. Everyone is playing against the dealer. If the dealer loses, everyone who hasn't already lost wins. It's a social game, unlike Texas Hold-Em where you can be up against any other player or the whole table at any time and then have to squint and keep perfectly still because they're trying to read your cards by your pores. Twenty-one is more festive and communal. Usually.

The smoking woman laughed then coughed, then laughed at the coughing and set it all in motion again. She looked at the dealer's six and waved her hand over her cards like they were safe sliding home.

At second base, Baldy-braids looked at his hole card, cringed, then saw the dealer's shit card and said, "No Card."

I looked at my down card and saw a jack of clubs. "A black jack," I said without thinking.

"Turn it over," said the dealer, a buxom middle-aged woman with too much eyeshadow.

I turned the card over and got another yellow chip and a blue one to boot.

Hydyn looked at his card and then squinted his eyes at the dealer and the deck, who rolled their eyes. If you've never seen playing cards roll their eyes, you've missed something. He waited a long time to make a decision, which made the table-mates very nervous but gave me a chance to look him over.

The name fit. He was a Utahn, a clean-cut white male, auburn hair, combed eyebrows, nice suit. He could be a lawyer. Oh, right. He was young and seemed a little lost out here in the big world. Like I said, a Utahn.

"Hit me," he said.

The smoker gasped in horror, then coughed. Comb-over stared with disbelief.

The dealer gave Hydyn a king.

"Can't win them all," he said and flipped over a five. He'd hit on a fourteen.

The coughing grew worse, more malicious. Baldy shook his streaks from side to side as the dealer flipped over a jack for sixteen and then put a five on top of that to get twenty-one. Everyone but me was busted.

"You took her break card," rasped the smoker.

"If you're going to play anchor, you should know how to play," said Follicle Boy.

Hydyn put three black chips in front of him.

I studied the colors. Yellows were twenty bucks, greens twenty-fives, blacks hundreds. Purples, which Hydyn had a few of, were five hundreds. A quick estimate suggested he had close to ten thousand dollars in front of him.

I left my twenty there.

A cocktail waitress appeared. I ordered a Chivas and soda. Vodka and cranberry for the lady, Denial Hairloss a heineken. Hydyn a diet coke with lemon.

More coughing.

We played four hands before the drinks came. I'd survived them all, and my original twenty-dollar chip sat just sat where I'd dropped it and I was a hundred ten dollars up. I was feeling pretty good. Winning was fun. This could be addicting.

Leather-Lungs and Hairnet were about the same as when I sat down, but Hydyn had lost every hand.

Our drinks came. I tipped the waitress a five from my wallet. Everyone else put chips on her tray.

Hydyn put four purples in front of him. I left my twenty.

"Mister," said Baldilocks, "you can't keep chasing a lost cause. Don't keep making a mistake because you've been making it for a long time. Throwing good money after bad is a fast way to have no money at all."

"This isn't your night," agreed the woman.

"I know what I'm doing," Hydyn said. "Do you really think I care about losing all this?"

"Looks to me like you're chasing to get even," said the mangy mane. "You've been doing it all night. You in deep, son?"

The dealer hesitated to start the next hand. I read it as a charitable gesture, giving Hydyn an opportunity to get out with the couple grand he still had.

"You're really not very good at this game," coughed the woman. "Maybe you should try slots."

"Or going home."

"Deal the cards or I'll call the boss over," he said.

I saw the dealer glance at the pit boss, who nodded back. Out came the cards.

Smoker got a jack, Coiffeur an eight, I got a king, Hydyn a six, and the dealer a four.

"Safe."

"No card."

"Blackjack!" I said and turned over the ace of diamonds.

"I'll split sixes," said Hydyn.

"Dammit," said the man with the comb-over. "You're anchor, son. Third base. She's showing a goddamn four! Are you—"

It was difficult to hear the last words because the smoker was in an asphyxiant fit of coughing. She stopped only after finishing her drink, which the waitress replaced before she could put it down. No-limit tables have very good bar service.

Here's the rule: if you have two of the same cards, like two sixes, you're allowed to turn them up and split them, allowing you play two hands. You have to match the bet. Hydyn did. He now had four thousand dollars in front of him.

The dealer put a ten on the first six.

"Okay, I see what you're doing," said the hairbrush refugee. "I apologize—"

"Hit me again," said Hydyn.

A queen.

The first hand was scooped with half his chips.

Strings of spit drooled from of the bald man's open mouth.

The dealer and smoker stared at Hydyn like he was committing hari-kari.

A nine hit the second six.

"Hit me again."

Coughing. Head palm.

It was a king.

He was busted.

The dealer turned over a jack, showing she had fourteen. Any one of the cards that Hydyn took would have busted her. She hit a six and stood at twenty and broke the others.

Hydyn signaled to the boss for more chips.

"Peppermill?" said the man to the smoker.

"Anywhere but here," she said.

They gathered their chips and left.

Another tray of clay money appeared in front of Hydyn, and I took my leave as well. To make the exodus complete, the dealer took a break, extending her hands front and back for the cringing over-head camera. I caught up to her just before she disappeared behind an unmarked door.

"Does he always play that well?" I asked.

She passed her ID over a sensor and I heard a click.

"Hydyn?"

"Yeah."

"I heard he used be play crazy and get really lucky. Now he just plays crazy."

"The casino backs him?"

"And comps him. He paid my salary for a month today."

"Who would—"

"Gotta go," she said. "Have a nice night." She slipped behind the door and I was alone.

I watch Hydyn feed the casino more money. Several new players found the table but didn't stay long. One hand at twenty dollars and they were off to the buffet.

Third base, or anchor, at a twenty-one table should be a strong player. It's the last chance before the dealer to take a card. A good third baseman will keep an eye on the table and have a feel for the deck. If he's a card counter, even better, but he should at least recognize when the dealer is in a weak position. Hydyn did none of this. Granted, the element of chance is never removed, but what I'd just witnessed was bar none the worse blackjack play I'd ever seen. And he did it in the face of stern advice from the other players. No wonder the casino gave him credit and comps. He was a walking hemorrhaging wallet.

I had a working theory now. Hydyn wasn't going anywhere. He'd won a hand. I cashed out and found a message for me at reception. Eliza was in the cafe.

I found her in a far back booth, a plate of untouched onion rings and a soft drink in front of her. She'd cleaned up her face, but her eyes were still swollen and red.

"Gambling problem?" I said sitting down.

"How bad is he losing?"

"It'd ruin my whole decade. For a lawyer, probably only a week. Maybe two."

"Was he playing well? Could you tell?"

"No and yes, I could tell. He's reckless as all hell."

"All hell?"

"All of it."

That made her smile.

"Mind if I have one?" meaning the onion rings.

"You can have them all."

They were cold but good. I glanced at my watch. It was still there.

"What now?" I asked.

"I guess we go home," she said.

"Do you want me to take pictures of him?" I heard myself say. "You know, for the divorce."

"Divorce?" she said as if tasting the word for the first time. "I won't divorce him."

"Oh. Okay. Good. You two should work it out."

"Work it out?" I think she was in shock. Not for the gambling, but for that word.

"How long has this been going on?"

"The gambling? I've suspected for years. It's gotten bad this last couple of years."

"And it's hurting your finances?"

"I wanted to go back to work, anyway."

"That's one way to handle this," I said. "Another might be an intervention backed with a threat of divorce."

"I can't divorce him."

"Why?"

"We're married."

"A divorce would take care of that."

"We've been together for so long," she said.

I thought of the line about chasing mistakes. Throwing good money after bad.

"He'll make it right," she said stiffening up. "He always has. If he doesn't win it back, he'll find it some other way. Besides, we have an inheritance coming."

That put a shiv through me.

That little line fit right into the knickknack case. Maybe Mrs. Dewinter was right to suspect murder by kitsch removal. Also, what the hell was I doing stirring the shit for a domestic case?

"Ready to go home?" I said, finishing the last onion ring.

"Sure."

"Are you going to pay me?"

She looked shocked.

"I said I would."

"Looks like you're going to be a little tight this week."

"Where is he?" she said.

I pointed to the casino floor. "The back twenty-one table."

She got up left the room. The waitress dropped a bill off and I paid it.

As I was finishing up, Eliza appeared from the hall. Her back was straight, and her eyes were firm. She handed me two green chips. I gave her back her ring.

CHAPTER EIGHT

"So you keep him around because you have sentimental attachment?"

"I keep him around because he's my husband."

"Which is officially a sentimental position."

"I don't think you can put it in those terms," she said. "Plus it's really none of your business."

"You're right."

We were again on I-80, eastbound now, heading to Bountiful.

"Wait," Eliza said. "You're asking this about your other case, aren't you? I almost forgot."

"I can't disclose that."

"Let us guess."

"Let us not."

"Twenty questions?"

"Do you smoke?" I asked.

"No. Wait. I'm supposed to ask the questions."

"Have you or your husband ever done anything that could be investigated by the Utah bar association for unethical behavior?"

That shut her up.

"No," she said after a deliberate pause.

"Spiffy."

"Should I be worried?"

"It's the twenty-first century. The American empire is collapsing, the environment has gone to shit, and no one is telling us when the McRib will return. There's plenty to worry about."

"Is that supposed to be funny?"

"Amusing. A clever turn of phrase and biting social commentary. The kind of thing that usually gets me a chuckle."

"Are we being investigated?"

I realized I'd gone overboard in my deflection. Now she was worried about their jobs and, worse, she wasn't laughing at my jokes.

"I can't comment," I said. "But if the bar wants to know about Hydyn, I'll tell them it's a family matter and you have it under control."

"Really? That's it?"

"You do have it under control, right?"

"Oh yes. That's all you'll say?"

"I might recommend his parents be fined for spelling his name that way."

No laugh. Maybe I'd hit a nerve. What's with Utahns and their spellings? Do other states do that? I'd like to know. Write the author if you see it happening in other places. He'll pass the message on to me.

After a while she leaned her seat back and fell asleep.

I was glad she did. She could have come at me with a barrage of questions I'd just have to fifth my way through, like how her sister and brother-in-law are involved in their supposed legal problems. And what does smoking have to do with anything?

Here was my thinking about why I'd asked both Eliza and Jennifer about smoking. What if they needed a new ashtray? They might have taken their grandmother's thing, as valuable as she said it was, because smokers don't really give a shit about who they inconvenience for their habit. I've watched too many butts being throw out car windows and floating in lakes to have any other opinion.

Not my best theory, I admit, but what could I do? Really, the stolen thing could fit in a pocket. If it had been taken, already it could have been sold, lost, destroyed, traded, mutated, ingested, recycled and turned into soup cans. It hadn't been in Eddie's garbage, but it might be in Hydyn Hunsing's. How was I to find out? And really, what kind of a stupid name is that?

These were the bullshit thoughts that carried me across the desert to Bountiful suburbia, where I gently awoke Eliza and watched her go inside.

My hangover was gone, and I needed a real meal. I ordered a

pizza and picked it up on the way home.

If there's a definitive line between divorcee, bachelor, and deadbeat, it might be measured in pizza boxes. There was a time when I cooked. I got onto a gourmet kick, lived on butter and cream for a couple of months, then curry and chickpeas. Haggis was a one-off as was blood pudding. That island is messed up. I ended up making three hundred pounds of my own pasta and putting on twenty pounds before I donated the pasta, not the weight, to the free kitchen that chucked it the trash when I couldn't prove restaurant standards of hygiene. To them I was just another fat pasta pusher.

Where was I? Pizza boxes.

Pizza is the perfect comfort food. Hot bread and cheese and grease. God, is there anything as good? Perfect for divorcees examining their lives, bachelors envying the divorcees for having had a relationship, and deadbeats envying the bachelors for washing. The first would do two pizzas a week, the second one, and the third would have a mozzarella IV stuck into their neck for four or more. Today's little trip to the pizza man was my third that week. I'd beaten the odds by buying two pizzas every visit so I'd have leftovers. I'm no loser.

Having measured my life single, married, and divorced, I've come to the sexist conclusion that women are the domesticators of men. Left on our own, we decorate in space ships, eat nothing but junk food, and masturbate so often it's a miracle we can even see. It's like civilization coming to the jungle, clothes and manners, forks and dishes cleaned the day they were dirtied. Egads! Granted, I don't understand hand towels people aren't actually allowed to use in guest bathrooms, but the rest of the civilizing effort is what keeps us from eating mud. One of these days I'll be in a position to ask a woman what it is men bring to the equation. I hope it's more than sperm donor. No one likes to think automation could take their job.

I suddenly felt threatened by a turkey baster.

Pizza in hand, pepperoni, jalapeño, and onion in mouth, I walked my feet down to basement and to behold my stuff.

Ehhh.

I went back upstairs for a drink, but my friends had cleaned me out. What pals. All I had left were bitters and Rose's lime juice. Thus was a new low point in my life.

I fired up my computer to make a list of pawn shops in the city. There were a lot, but they were clustered together, at least linearly. Eighty percent of them were along State Street, a central artery next to Main Street, which didn't have as many pawn shops. I didn't think pawn shop people would buy the story that the tin ashtray was worth big bucks, but I thought maybe they might remember the guy who tried to sell them that story. Then again, maybe they had put money out for it. Then it would be worse. I'd get to accuse some bare-armed bald mustachioed bruiser of accepting stolen goods. Either way, I'd have to schlep to dozens of seedy shops. Put in shoe leather. Real detective work is a lot of schlepping and a lot of footwork. It's not a very fun part of the job, so I tended not to do it.

I surfed on over to eBay to find out what knock-off plastic Amish rockers were going for with and without LEDs. I had three in different stages of completion. Yes, it was a phase. My life is a series of phases.

There wasn't even a subcategory for them. I lost a little faith in the internet then and fought the urge to surf to less reputable sites, wondering if Rule 34 extended to flashing furniture.

For shits and giggles, I searched '1876 Philadelphia Expo souvenirs,' and Zeus himself alighted upon my shoulder. There was a picture of a bullshit tin ashtray with a bullshit date 1876 scratched on it. Asking price, $10,000. Reserve had not been met.

I mentioned automation taking away jobs before. Private investigator is in serious jeopardy to Google bots. There it was. The clue, the connection, the culmination. All I had to do was find out who was running the auction and the case was solved. I'd leave the domestic fallout to Dewinter and Dewinterites. It bothered me, though. Two days, a set of clothes, and hundreds of miles later, the only real clue I had was from a three-second computer search. I told myself that it was my keen detective senses that led me to make the search. I tell myself a lot of things to get through the day.

The user name for the auction was someguy9661. I stared at the numbers trying to match them up to what numbers I had on my suspects—addresses, number of wives, limbs, and then searched on someguy9960 and someguy9662, both of whom existed and had higher rankings. I surmised it was an anonymous automatically assigned number after a lame name. Automation can work for the bad guys too.

I noticed that someguy9661 had recently sold a Llardró statuette, two glass paperweights, and an assortment of hotel soaps. Also, as Amelia had mentioned missing, there was a thimble and a silver collector's spoon. Here at least was proof that it wasn't Mrs. Dewinter's dead husband, Verne, beckoning her into the light.

Having seen that the shipper was in Utah and wanted $9.99 for delivery, I sent a private message. I will be in Utah this week and would like to save the $9.99 and pick it up. Would someone willing to pay ten big ones shirk at ten normal for shipping? I added, I'd also like to verity its authenticity. I'll pay in cash.

The second line might spook him, maybe, but I knew the third line would net him. In-person cash transactions go around protective channels and policies. Getting a refund would be hell on me. But here's a spoiler: I wasn't actually going to buy it!

I sent the message and waited for a response. None immediately came. I shouldn't have expected one. It was two in the morning.

I checked one more time for "old-timey plastic furniture" and then went to bed.

I spent the morning again trying to arrange my things into the binary worlds of "I can't live without this" and "even under pain of torture I can't come up with a single good reason I still have this." There was no middle ground. You can guess my progress.

I spent the afternoon trying to minimize the "I can't live without this" pile into essences. Could I recall my bowling hobby with one ball instead of three? Did I need to keep all my Pogs, or would a cross-section be enough?

That had been a short hobby, Pogs. By the time I held and admired all two hundred of them, some rare mature bone in my head told me I didn't need any of them. I'd forgotten what the allure had been. I'd started collecting way after they were popular, long after the fad had died its sudden but well-deserved death. They were dumb, but I seem to remember dropping more than a little money on them at a time when I had more than a little money. I could eBay them. It's where most had come from.

There's the wrinkle—even if the sentimental value was gone, the material value might remain. Did I throw good effort after bad at trying to recoup investment? I couldn't see myself running internet auctions for cardboard circles. Maybe I could sell them as a lot.

That night, I went online looking at collectible Pogs. My collection was a joke compared to some I saw. A couple were being sold by the pound. They were good deals. I was about to put in a bid, when I got a notice that I had a new private message.

Like a Narcan shot, I caught myself about to drop fifty bucks on sixty pounds of Pogs. Saved from another terrible life choice, I closed the tab and went to my messages.

Someguy9661 wrote. That would be acceptable. I would prefer a public place for obvious reasons. You with so much cash and me with such a valuable item. I'm available tomorrow. I'll hold it that long.

The clutter close call had my adrenaline pulsing. My mind was sharp for once. I took a moment to think about this. Both suspects had seen me. If they saw me at the meeting, I'd be made and they'd be off. I had to catch them with the item and that wouldn't happen if they fled upon seeing my cottony brown eyes. I could report to Mrs. Dewinter, but it would be their word against mine. I'm sure she'd believe me, but I suspected she was really looking for material to show the real judges: her granddaughters.

I looked around the room for inspiration and lit upon the empty tipped schnapps bottle and came up with a plan.

CHAPTER NINE

"Are we getting paid for this?" asked Critter.

"No."

"Then why the fuck are we doing this?" said Dara.

"Because you said there's nothing to do in January," said I. "Well? Here's something."

"He has us there," said Garrett.

I'd arranged to have the gang meet me at the Snowbird ski resort up Little Cottonwood Canyon. Snowbird is probably the most famous of the Utah ski resorts. Among that odd breed of nutcases who like winter sports involving steep inclines and suffocating snow, Snowbird is renowned for high prices and, consequently, an exclusive vibe. Most locals ski elsewhere. Tourists with money ski Snowbird, and as I understand it, they have a good time. Again though, I have little insight into the fucked-up brain patterns of winter sports enthusiasts. I've long suspected early childhood trauma with a snow cone fetish as the undiagnosed reasoning, but I didn't get the grant to follow up on that.

I'd sent Perry inside to get the tickets. I didn't know if my quarry was here yet and didn't want to take the chance of being recognized. Not wanting anyone to associate the gang with each other, I had us huddled together outside in a parking lot.

It was cold. January in Utah is cold by custom. Up in the mountains, where skiing and snowboarding happens and people go out of their way NOT to shovel snow away—sometimes even making it themselves!—cold is just the beginning of what it was. Had the sun been shining, it would have been warmer. That's what the sun does. It might have clawed above minus five then. Whoopee. As it was overcast, we had ten degrees of frost over a new layer of fresh powder laid down the day before. Whoopee.

I pride myself in going all winter without using a coat. Since my outdoor adventures are usually confined to car to bar and back again, it's an accessory I just don't need to be hassled with. Hats, gloves, scarves, boots, or socks warmer than canvas were other things I've kind of let go. Those things I got rid of, but Pogs ...

I'd dug up an old pair of ski pants that didn't fit as well as they did in college when I tried the sport for an entire day. I had a newly purchased black hat on my head. No gloves, no scarf. Tennis shoes. I did, however, have my son's favorite snowboard.

Standard was the best decked out. He had skis and matching boots, gloves, a hat with a ball on top, and yellow goggles. The cotton hoodie didn't help, though. Nor did the jeans.

"You know only total idiots ski in jeans," Dara told him.

"I'm not going to ski for real."

"But you'll stand out as an idiot."

"I won't."

"Lots of people ski in jeans," said Garrett.

"And all of them get mocked mercilessly."

"Like you'd know."

"What do other people care if someone else skis in jeans?"

"It's territorial," I said. "It shows who doesn't belong on the slopes. A tribal thing."

"And you'll freeze your ass off," Dara said. "Once cotton get wet, it doesn't dry. It freezes."

Dara was dressed in jeans, too, but she didn't have ski props. She could be a sightseer just there for the view. Garrett, the same. Critter, after much arguing and convincing, had agreed to go under cover as a mitten.

Perry strolled out of the building, waving the tickets. He had on wool pants straight from an Army/Navy surplus store. He'd remembered boots. Hiking boots, but still boots. For a top layer, he'd brought his secret weapon: a black windbreaker that said 'Security' on the back in big yellow letters. It was better than a passkey to get into places.

I looked at my watch. "Time to get into position."

"This is a real sting, then?" said Standard. "Like, cop stuff?"

"Yes. Cop-like stuff."

"Okay. It's real. Nice," he said. "Count me in. I'm alpha go."

"You're alpha go, Stan?" said Dara. "Will you still be alpha go after you hump a couple klicks to recon the DMZ for bogies?"

"It's a term," he said. "This kind of operation should be run like a military exercise, with pinpoint precision. Am I right, Tony?"

I wanted to say that if I needed pinpoint precision this would be the last group I'd call together. We're not exactly reliable.

"Sure," I said.

The plan was to make the exchange on Snowbird's famous aerial tram, a floating cable car that lifts people three thousand feet over a mile and half in just ten minutes. It runs all year—in the summer for the mountain views and hiking, in the winter to spread disease and slush. And skiers.

This was to be the public place to make the deal. Dara would play the buyer. I figured her small frame would be the least threatening to the thief and they would let her examine the knickknack without demanding that she let them see the money.

I would be as close as possible, recording the transaction on my phone. I would not be recognized because—and here's really why I chose this high altitude freezer for the deal—I'd be in a ski mask! There are not many places in the world where someone in a ski mask does not draw attention. In fact, I could think of only one. Skiing. Or in my case, carrying my son's snowboard.

In case the tram was too crowded and I couldn't get close enough to get the incontrovertible video evident, I had Standard, Garrett and Critter backing me up on their phones. Perry would be up at the top, ready to step in as "Security" when the tram unloaded if things got weird.

The only problem would be catching the right tram. They came and went about every ten minutes. We agreed to be on the two o'clock one, but that was before I knew how frequent and non-scheduled they were. The last time I was on this thing it was summertime, and then the trams went on the hour and the half. Who could have guessed they'd get more use in winter?

We took our positions in the waiting area. Perry took an earlier tram to be in position at the top.

I pulled down my mask and hid my shoes behind the snow-board.

I tried to see a familiar face but the place was packed with skiers. The faces I could see were behind sunglasses or goggles, under hats and above scarves.

"Alpha go, alpha go, alpha go." Standard stared into the distance, psyching himself up.

"We should separate," I whispered. "Draw less attention."

"Good idea," said Critter as mitten.

Standard stayed in the zone while the rest of us mingled.

Again, I couldn't see anyone I knew or even anyone looking for anyone. State memory kicked in and I a recalled a night during high school waiting at a table for an hour eating nachos and watching the door before the manager suggested to me that maybe I'd been stood up. He'd felt sorry for me but not so much that he didn't charge me for the nachos.

The tram slid into the garage and emptied.

It was two minutes past two. This had to be it. Time to board.

Worry and re-lived disappointment tensed me up and I felt like the boss had just asked me into his office at the end of my shift, the last day of the month. Stan might be in the zone—alpha go—ready to hot-wire a boxcar, but emotionally I was preparing for failure.

The doors shut and the tram lurched. I found myself not at all near Dara.

Amid curses and bumps and ugly glares, I moved around the car until I could see my friends. Unburdened by tragic blind dates, they'd remembered the plan and were prepared. Standard had his camera out and was taking a selfie. Critter filmed through the window while Garrett kept his eye on Dara. I dug out my phone.

"Is some guy here?" Dara said.

The tram fell quiet, the few low conversations muting at the strange request.

"I said I'm looking for some guy. Are you here?"

There had to be thirty people in there. Belly to belly, ski to ass. No one moved. My guts churned.

Dads pulled a note from her pocket. "Some guy 9661," she read.

"Is this some kind of sick game, young lady?" said a woman. "To go ninety-six with a sixty-one year old?"

The woman talking was in her forties, someone I didn't know. Her matching winter garb also matched that worn by three teenagers I assumed to be her children. Her comment spoke of prudishness and a poor understanding of sexual positions.

I saw a grin creep over Dara's face, slow and building, like a phaser overloading. I cringed and shrank back, wondering if I should turn off my recording before the verbal beat-down. Less evidence of the emotional trauma my foul-mouthed friend was about to unleash on the tourist.

"I'm some guy," came a voice.

Dara turned to look at the man, surprised, ready to fire.

"Oh, well, why the fuck didn't you say anything before?" she said.

It was Eddie. I lifted up my camera to get a good shot of his face. Dara's strange behavior had opened up a little space around her. The prude threw her chin up in a huff.

"Can I see the fucking thing?" Dara asked. Loudly. She'd been trained in theatre and could project so the cheap seats could hear her even if they didn't want to.

Eddie glanced around to see if anyone was looking at them. Everyone was.

He gestured and Hydyn walked over. I don't know how I missed either of them. Eddie was wearing an old peacoat and Hydyn a long blended winter trench.

Hydyn reached in his pocket and passed Eddie something silver.

The entire tram watched him do it.

Hydyn noticed, cleared his throat and pulled up his collar.

Eddie handed the object to Dara.

"Well, look at this fucking thing," she said. "Hey, bitch, this is what I came here for." She held the ashtray up to show her, giving me a perfect picture of it, Dara, and the two grandsons-in-law.

"Gotcha!" I yelled and stepped forward—well, actually more like pushed my way forward, nearly knocking over a couple people.

For dramatic effect, I tossed the snowboard to the floor and then with a flourish, careful to make sure Critter got my good side, I pulled off my mask.

"It's the shitty worm guy," said Eddie.

"It's the guy who took all my good cards. Did you drive my wife to Wendover?"

"It is I," said I, "Tony Flaner, private investigator, and you two have some explaining to do. When Grandma finds out about this …"

Hydyn the lawyer, no doubt employing the hard-won knowledge he'd gathered for his Juris Doctorate degree, shut the fuck up then and there. I never heard another syllable come out of his lips. Not to this day.

Eddie was not so cool. He got what some aquatic scientists call crazy eyes. It was an alarming look, the visage of consciousness searching fantasy for answers and finding only Mountain Dew hangovers.

But wait. He grabbed the snowboard off the floor and held it up like a club.

Dara jumped back. "You wouldn't fucking hit a girl would you, you asshole?"

"See you in hell!" Eddie yelled and swung my son's favorite snowboard into the window. It shattered. So did the window.

I'd seen this before, I realized. Eddie had lived it.

"No Eddie!" I screamed. "Don't be an idiot! Don't jump!"

But it was too late. He'd already swung a leg over the side. He gave a salute to us and then, for effect, because a good line is good more than once, said, "See you in Hell!"

A blur brushed past, yellow-eyed and alpha go, but Standard was too late.

Eddie flew spread-eagle off the tram into a hundred-foot free fall and landed on his face in a snow drift.

A pair of skiers saw the fall and veered off to mark where to look for the body, but just as they got there Eddie's hand popped up out of Snowbird's famously deep powder. He'd be okay. Stupidity, in this case, wasn't a fatal condition.

You might expect everyone in the car to have cheered or breathed a sigh of relief, but really we were all just stunned and confused.

I think I was the first person to say, "huh," but it caught on and traveled the car like gossip before someone else said, "A little help here, please."

We all turned and looked at the window Eddie had bashed out and leaped from. We could see the bottom of Standard's ski boot, which seemed strange. No Standard to be seen.

Garrett appeared beside me. He took the mitten off his arm, and Critter gasped for air like he'd been suffocating. Dara handed me the ashtray. Hydyn was hiding in some corner.

"Help." It was a soft sound coming from outside.

I moved to the window and poked my head out. There was Standard upside down hanging on the side of the tramcar, moving softly in the breeze like sweet autumn aspen leaves.

"Hey, Stan," said Garrett.

"Hi."

"We got the fuckers," said Dara.

"Alpha go," said Standard softly. "Hoorah."

"Yep," I agreed. "Hey wait. You didn't drop your phone, did you?"

"Oh no. I got it right here." He struggled to pull his arm back and show his camera. It was still recording.

"Good job."

Garrett said, "If you fall, try to shield it with your body so it won't break. It's hard to get data off a broken phone."

"You got yours, didn't you?" I asked Critter.

"The framing might have been off," said the puppet. "It was hard to see in there."

I looked at my own recording. It was okay, but it wouldn't be as clear as Standard's, who'd had the best view.

"Help."

"What? Oh right. Sorry, Standard. Help's on its way."

"What's the plan?"

"The tram's coming up to the top. All you have to do is … hang around."

"Fucking Flaner. That's beneath even you," said Dara.

"Really?"

"Yes," came the cry from outside. "Total shit joke. You're losing it."

"Critter?"

The puppet just stared and curled its lip up. Garrett shook his head in shame.

"Okay," I said and leaned out the window. "How's this—"

I didn't get the chance to try another one. In leaning over, I'd brushed the boot, which pulled the jeans, and dropped my friend into the snow which was then only five feet below the tram.

A minute later, we pulled into the mountain-top platform. The doors opened and the skiers poured out to do their crazy snow stuff.

When the crowd was gone, two people stood in the waiting area to take the ride down: Eliza and Jennifer. I took a picture of their shocked faces as they recognized me and counted only one of their husbands still on the tram.

CHAPTER TEN

Only about half of my hoard was collections. That was good, I thought. The other half was hobbies that required me to do something. Like weave or carve, paint or hike. I don't know why that mattered, but somehow I took heart in that and hoped to use that insight to winnow out my stuff.

I was having no luck.

I kept thinking about Mrs. Dewinter, Amelia as she required me to address her. She lived in a museum of her own life. Or not. They were knickknacks, not souvenirs. Most of her things she couldn't tell me where she got them. When I'd pressed her, I learned that most had no real sentimental value for her at all. It was just something she'd picked up.

She at least displayed them, though. I was here wrestling with values of things in boxes that I hadn't touched or thought about in years. Yes, there's that rule again. If you haven't touched it or thought of it in two years, you don't need it. Looking at all my stuff and having memories of all of it—good, bad, specific, general—I thought that was a pretty arbitrary rule, something made up by a pop culture self-help guru on daytime television. Maybe to sell a book.

The one thing I was known for, at least by those people who knew me beyond my accumulation of hobbies, was my ever-changing career path. I now called myself a detective. How long would that last? I wasn't sure. I'd solved one big case, one medium case, and a bunch of stalkings. I felt good about this one, but who was I fooling? If a shiny squirrel ran by my window right then, I'd be a cyber-rodent wrangler in a second.

I decided not to think about it. The usual tides of my life, the push and the pull, the paths of least resistance, would come again and I'd go with it or fight it. Fighting it had been surprisingly satisfying. I hoped it would stay that way.

In the meantime, I tried to figure out what of my old life belonged in my new.

I thought about Amelia's change of heart when the case was busted open. A mix of pragmatism, sentimentality and defeat.

"You were right," I'd begun. "You were being robbed by your grandchildren."

"Which one?" She'd narrowed her eyes.

I glanced at Charlie, wondering how I could use him as a human shield if she went at me.

"All of them," I said.

"What?"

I'd brought a messenger bag. It's like a big purse. Mine was green canvas and made to look like it'd seen action in Korea when in fact it had only seen sweatshops in China. What an advance. I felt bad about the bag. It should have been a briefcase, something I could lay down on the table and open with a smart click to show how professional I was. But of course I'd probably need to dress better than an open Hawaiian shirt and 501s. Whatever.

I presented Amelia first with the ashtray. The bait.

She took it, looked and passed it to Charlie who took it, looked, and passed it back to me. I put on the coffee table.

Next came the screenshots from eBay.

"Is this the missing Llardró?"

"Yes, that's it."

"Do you recognize these?" I showed her pictures of the paperweights.

She gasped. Her eyes flashed around the shelves. I assumed she was looking for them, or rather where they had been. "I hadn't even noticed."

Then came the hotel soaps.

Another gasp, which surprised me because you'd think she'd be ready for the next one.

"Ten of them?" said Charlie. "Did you notice they were missing?"

"No. And I'm glad I didn't," said Mrs. Dewinter—Amelia.

"I'd have been beside myself. They're priceless."

"No. Only about twenty bucks without shipping," I said.

She scowled. "To me they were priceless."

And she hadn't noticed ten of them missing. I guess it made sense in this cluttered place.

I showed her the spoon and thimble. A tear was in her eye.

"What did the statue go for?" she asked.

"That one got five-fifty," I said.

"Who was doing this?"

"I told you. Your grandchildren."

"Which one?"

"All of them," I said. "Eddie and Jennifer, Hydyn—God, what a spelling—and Lizzie. They were all in on it."

"Jennifer and Lizzie knew?"

"Yes," I said patiently, allowing for the shock. "They all did."

And here I pulled out the photos from the tram. I was going to use my computer, show her video, but Walgreens was having a sale of photo prints, and I thought it would more professional. She could have something to keep. You know, as a souvenir of her family's demolition. I put in on the expense list. It was a bargain. Really. You gotta watch the sales.

She looked from one photo to the next to the next to the next, rearranging them and starting over as if they might have changed from the shuffling. She held a long time on one of her granddaughter's surprised faces.

"Why were they doing it?" asked Charlie. "It was just for some quick bucks, right?"

I heard his concern about Amelia's horrific premonition that this had all been done to send her to an earlier grave.

"Eddie and Jenni, for sure," I said. "A couple hundred can really help them. Eddie has a serious video game habit and has run up micro transactions on his credit card that would make a teenager blush. He has to hide his statements at the bottom of his trashcan to keep it from his wife. This I know."

"Jennifer?" Amelia's question was nearly a whisper.

"She didn't know about his continuing problem, but I'm sure she suspected. She's been unhappy with how he's not doing anything with his life, and they're still recovering from older bills."

"Hydyn and Lizzie?" Her voice was stronger.

Here I knew I was on sensitive ground. My feeling was that Amelia's fear was correct in their case. They needed the inheritance.

On the tram ride down, Jennifer had told me that it was Hydyn's idea to take the Llardó and then the ashtray. "Because they'd be missed."

Lizzie hadn't contradicted her.

I looked at Hydyn. But he kept his mouth shut. He shook his head vigorously, however, trying to shut up the rest of them.

"Eddie needed the money," said Lizzie, forgetting that she had the same motivation. "Those things weren't doing the old lady any good."

"Hydyn's debts are a million times worse," Jennifer said, well, spat really.

This family had issues.

"Both your husbands are jerks," I said, "if you don't mind me saying."

"We don't mind."

"Neither one of you has kids. You're both young and attractive, smart and employed. Why not dump their sorry asses?"

"Where angels fear to tread, Tony," warned Critter.

The suspects all looked at Garrett, still unsure about the puppet.

He was right, though. I should stay out of it.

With the attention on him, Garrett said, "So you guys going to divorce?"

"Absolutely not," they said.

I looked at Amelia and said, "Hydyn and Lizzie needed money too." I left out that the money they'd been angling for was in her will, not on her wall.

Charlie said, "What do you want to do about this?"

"Police?" said Amelia.

Charlie nodded. I nodded. She stared.

"This isn't going to split them up, by the way," I told her. "I confronted them with this. Since they're all involved, there's really no new fault to see. And frankly, I suspect even if your granddaughters hadn't been in on it, and this was all a new revelation, they'd stick to their marriages."

"Why?" asked Charlie.

Amelia was deep in thought.

"They're literally married to their mistakes," I said.

Habit is a bitch.

Amelia looked around her living room, her eyes flashing on statues and tchotchkes. Knickknacks a plenty.

"I wish it had been Verne," she said softly.

Charlie and I shared a glance and a sigh.

"You've done good work, Tony," she said.

"I wish I'd brought you better news."

"Like what?" asked Charlie.

"That the things had been mislaid. That a cat had taken them or a neighborhood kid during a scavenger hunt. One with a lock-pick kit, maybe."

Amelia nodded.

"It's all junk. It's going to be theirs anyway. Why wait? It's not doing me any good. It might them."

The echo of Lizzie's comment was surprising. So was the idea that they weren't doing her any good. She loved them. These things, as many and as varied as they were, were part of her. Her soaps were dear friends, the Tibetan bell a companion. This woman lived alone except for these things.

A wiser man or a better detective would have kept their mouth shut. Not me. Like arguing for others' divorces, I stepped into this one right quick. "But the sentimental value is something. Don't underestimate that."

"I should use things and love people," she said. "Not the other way around."

"Damn, that's good," I said.

"Thank you again, Tony. Charlie. I think I want to be alone."

I took my bill with itemized expenses, including a credit for the money I'd won in Wendover, but not the thousand—that was another case—and left it with the other stuff. I'd included a note saying that if the bill was too far out of line we could talk about it.

At the door, she called me back.

"Tony. Here I want you to have this." She held the ashtray out to me. "For a souvenir."

The last thing I needed was another thing. I took it.

As Charlie closed the door, we heard the first soft sobs coming from the inside. Charlie drove me home.

Amelia paid my bill in full by money order that week. I put the ashtray on my desk. There was already a mounted finger trap on the wall. It seemed like a good place for it.

Randy wasn't half as mad at me for breaking his snowboard as I'd thought he'd be. He said he'd never actually used it. He had it in his room in case his friends came over. I bought him a new one. Amelia helped. I think he took pity on me because he saw how upset I'd been at losing it. He'd hugged me and said the new one was better. I don't know shit from snowshoes, so he might have been lying.

My kid's pretty great.

My friends have different attitudes about their Snowbird adventure. Dara says I need to stop taking advantage of our friendship to do the heavy work of my new "short-lived" job. Garrett said it was exciting. Perry thought it drew unwanted attention. Standard threatened to sue me and the resort and the tram makers and the jeans company and Mrs. Dewinter. That lasted about a day, and then he started working on a comedy routine about the experience.

My friends are pretty okay.

I folded the cardboard flaps back into a lid and pushed the box to a wall.

I had the space. That was the final conclusion. I'd removed the more obvious pieces of garbage—yes, the terrarium—and the rest of it could sit, ignored, in the dark of my new house, out of sight in the basement until hell freezes over or I need the space or otherwise have to face it again. When I die, it'll be left to my heirs to deal with. Maybe they'll sell my stuff on the internet, maybe they'll haul it all away in a truck to the dump, but I blessedly won't be there to see it.

Or I'll have to deal with it later, like when I need the room or otherwise have to face it.

Upstairs was neat-ish. Livable. Company wouldn't gasp and run away in horror, as long as I kept up with the pizza boxes and garbage pickups, changed the vacuum bags once in a while, used the vacuum, wiped the counters. Dust. Maybe.

What stuff, what parts of my history could I live without? All of it. None of it.

THANKS

Thank you for reading THE KNICKKACK CASE. Pretty great wasn't it? If you agree, you could do me a big favor by telling all your friends and giving it a review on Amazon and/or Goodreads. Reviews are really helpful. If you hated it, you can also leave a review. That's fair.

Look for more Tony Flaner mysteries at wonderful bookstores near you, real or the cyber kind.

Remember to compost.

ABOUT THE AUTHOR

Johnny Worthen is an award-winning, best-selling author of books and stories. Trained in stand-up comedy, modern literary criticism and cultural studies, he writes upmarket multi-genre fiction, symbolized by his love of tie-dye and good words. "I wear tie-dye for my friends, but I write what I like to read," he says. "This guarantees me at least one fan."

Johnny lives in Sandy, Utah, with his wife and sons.

Visit him at www.johnnyworthen.com

Made in the USA
Las Vegas, NV
02 March 2022